IMAGINE THAT

Licensed exclusively to Imagine That Publishing Ltd
Tide Mill Way, Woodbridge, Suffolk, IP12 1AP, UK
www.imaginethat.com
Copyright © 2015 Imagine That Group Ltd
All rights reserved
0 2 4 6 8 9 7 5 3 1
Manufactured in China

Written by Ellie Wharton
Illustrated by Maxine Lee

ISBN 978-1-78958-606-0

A catalogue record for this book is available from the British Library

Dilbert Dragon
AND THE
Magic Garden

Written by Ellie Wharton
Illustrated by Maxine Lee

Little Fairy had a lovely garden. It was full of flowers and butterflies and buzzing insects and trees and ponds and flowers.

Buzz, buzz!

Flutter, flutter!

But it wasn't just lovely ...

Little Fairy's garden was also magic!
And because it was magic it was full
of magical creatures – like Ned
the Leprechaun who told Little
Fairy all about the glittering pots
of gold hidden at the end of rainbows.

Or friendly Moss Monster
who loved to play hide-and-seek ...

Or White Unicorn who only appeared when there was a full moon and gave Little Fairy rides up and down the garden.

Gallop, gallop, gallop!

But sometimes the magic in Little Fairy's garden got a little out of hand, and today was one of those days.

Dilbert the Dragonfly had decided he didn't want to be a dragonfly any more. He was bored with being small ... he wanted to be a REAL dragon!

And because Little Fairy's garden was magic,
that's exactly what happened.

One moment Dilbert was very small and the next moment

he was ...

very,

very,

big.

Dilbert had changed into a dragon!

But strangely, Dilbert found he didn't like being big.
He couldn't dodge in and out of the trees like he used to ...

And when he took a drink of water from the pond he ended up swallowing every last drop ...

And what's more, every time Dilbert tried to speak flames came out of his mouth!

Soon poor Dilbert was flapping about in a panic and Little Fairy's magic garden was on fire!

Little Fairy didn't know what to do.
She had never met a dragon before,
never mind a dragonfly trying to be a dragon!

BIG FAIRY'S MAGIC FOREST

There was only one thing for it ... she would have to go
next door to Big Fairy's magic forest.

Big Fairy was more than happy to help.
Nothing had happened in her forest
for a very long time.

Big Fairy flew up to Dilbert and jumped on his back.
In fact, she was so big that Dilbert couldn't carry her
and they crashed to the ground.

While Dilbert was pinned to the floor, Little Fairy quickly flew up to him and whispered a magical spell.

Crash!

'He thinks he's small, just like a gnat
But flies as fast as any bat ...
And as for courage, he never lacks ...
So bring our brave old Dilbert back!'

WHHOOOOOOOOSHHH!

And Dilbert was back to his old, small self again.

Little Fairy and Big Fairy decided to have a party to celebrate. Dilbert was the smallest creature there.

Although he was small, Dilbert still felt very important, and he promised never to wish to be someone else again.